Ki...
Choose Y...

the

makes you feel like you are the author."

Jordan Blondin, age 9

"I think that these books are fantastic
and I'm amazed how many endings
there are."

AJ Lange, age 10

"They are super fun and super detailed!"

Ava Morey, age 9

"It's like a new book every time
I pick it up."

Quin Carpenter, age 9

CHOOSE YOUR OWN ADVENTURE®

CHOOSE YOUR OWN ADVENTURE®

SPIES: HARRY HOUDINI

KATHERINE FACTOR

ILLUSTRATED BY EOIN COVENEY
COVER ILLUSTRATED BY MIA MARIE OVERGAARD

CHOOSECO
WAITSFIELD, VERMONT

Book design: Stacey Boyd, Big Eyedea Visual Design

For information regarding permission, write to:

CHOOSECO
P.O. Box 46, Waitsfield, Vermont 05673
www.cyoa.com

ISBN-10: 1-937133-36-2
ISBN-13: 978-1-937133-36-8

Names: Factor, Katherine, author. | Coveney, Eoin, illustrator.
Title: Spies. Harry Houdini / Katherine Factor ; illustrated by Eoin
Coveney.
Other Titles: Harry Houdini | Choose your own adventure. Spies.
Description: Waitsfield, Vermont : Chooseco, [2020] | Interest age
level: 007-012. | Summary: "YOU are America's first celebrity superhero,
Harry Houdini, "The King of Cuffs." You have enchanted audiences across
the United States with your death-defying live escapes ... But one
follower of your act has a serious request: with all of your sleight of
hand and feats of strength and intelligence, will you, Harry Houdini,
become a spy to learn information abroad and help the United States?"--
Provided by publisher.
Identifiers: ISBN 1937133362 | ISBN 9781937133368
Subjects: LCSH: Houdini, Harry, 1874-1926--Juvenile fiction. |
Spies--United States--Juvenile fiction. | Escape artists--United
States--Juvenile fiction. | Spy stories. | CYAC: Houdini, Harry,
1874-1926--Fiction. | Spies--United States--Fiction. | Escape artists--
United States--Fiction. | LCGFT: Action and adventure fiction. | Choose-
your-own stories.
Classification: LCC PZ7.1.F335 Sph 2020 | DDC [Fic]--dc23

Published simultaneously in the United States and Canada

Printed in Canada

10 9 8 7 6 5 4 3 2 1

For my parents, Barbara and Lance,
for wonder infused with logic.

BEWARE and WARNING!

This book is different from other books. YOU and you alone are in charge of what happens in this story.

You are Harry Houdini, a street performer who dreams of becoming the most famous magician in the world. You have been dazzling audiences and provoking police across the United States with your edgy escape acts. But you dream of even bigger glory.

The year is 1899, and you are approached by the head of the U.S. Secret Service with a special mission. Will YOU, Harry Houdini, agree to use your sleight of hand talents and your enormous intelligence to travel abroad and spy for the United States? And maybe find international fame when you are there? Or will you stay in America to perfect your tricks, with the help of your wild and diverse friends from Coney Island and San Francisco? You will also make choices that determine YOUR own fate in the story. Choose carefully, because the wrong choice could end in disaster—even death. But don't despair. At any time, YOU can go back and make another choice, and alter the path of your fate . . . and maybe even history.

It is 1899. You are Erik Weisz, and you hail from Hungary but moved to America at age four. You are now called Harry Houdini. You named yourself after your hero, the grandfather of magic, Jean-Eugène Robert-Houdin.

Determined to become the "Greatest Magician of All Time," you are destined to become America's first superhero. You have intense features: glowing eyes that can laser-focus, and a muscular body. You are athletic, clever, and confident.

Like any magician of your era, you work your way through performance circuits, including the rough-and-tumble life of traveling sideshows. You have faced poverty and grueling hours, hoping for a big break. Your tricks include sleight of hand, cards, the "metamorphosis" box, and handcuff escapes, but you dream of bigger acts. You know every way to pick a lock from constantly working on your craft.

You hype yourself as "The King of Cuffs." "Who can lock up and trick the Supreme Ruler of all handcuffs?" you roar through towns and cities, beating your challengers every time. This stunt angers the cops and hurts local pride. It also draws the most news coverage, which is essential to becoming famous.

Turn to the next page.

2

This afternoon, you are in Chicago, performing in front of the Clark Street Museum, where you invited every police precinct to try their best locks on you. You have loved Chicago ever since learning tricks at the World's Fair a few years ago. Downtown dazzles with huge marble buildings. A large crowd gathers. The police seem agitated. That's just where you want them—a part of the entertainment.

A police officer steps forward, saying: "I am Lieutenant Andrew Rohan, I will lock you with the finest irons." He cuffs your wrists together. You enter your portable, stand-up curtain, then—in the blink of an eye—you emerge free! The crowd cries wildly. Yet something feels off. You have gotten this far on your instinct and showmanship . . . but you can't quite place what's wrong.

You begin to talk to adoring fans, when suddenly, *BLAM!* Rohan and his cops surround you.

Go on to the next page.

"You may have broken free, Houdini, but you are the amateur! You are performing in public without permission, without a license," the officers chide.

"C'mon, the act is over," you respond. "Cut it out!"

They grab you, shake you down in a search, yelling: "Where is the ring of keys?!" and arrest you. It takes three men to restrain you with chains. When you reach the main jail, you are slammed into a cold, damp cell. You use breathing techniques to stay calm and in control.

Turn to the next page.

4

You believe the permit charge is a false charge, but the police won't let you see a lawyer. Locked up for hours, desperately you scan for anything that might help you break free. You are not yet experienced at large escapes like a prison cell, having built your career with card tricks and box illusions. You suss out the window and the duct off the heating vent for any escape routes.

You stare out the tiny window, unsure of your future. Suddenly, a small bird flies in. A good omen. It sings, offering you some relief. You think quickly, yank a feather off the bird, and hide it in your sleeve.

Turn to page 6.

6

"Well, well, listen to me, Houdini." Lieutenant Rohan barges in, slamming the door and bolting it, ruining any chance of you overcoming him. "A great showman, are you? And now you're in a jam. But you may be able to do us a favor. Let's make a deal—your freedom in exchange for secret police training in your skills."

Rohan continues: "Be a good American. With so many criminals out there, we need skills like yours. For one, obviously you can train us in lock picking. You will be a hero—bigger than life!"

"Exactly how will I be a known hero if it is all secret training?"

"That will depend. The more we learn, the more arrests we can make. Aren't you tired of sweating for nothing in sideshows? If you say no . . . well, we'll find a way to keep ya locked in here!"

And with that threat, the Lieutenant leaves, slamming the door. You realize that you could deny his request and escape—maybe. This would give you amazing press and increase your name recognition to a nationwide scale. If it doesn't work, you could be seen as a failure or face real jail time.

Do you decide to try for an escape with the quill you took from the bird? If you give it your best shot, go on to the next page.

If you choose to give in to the police demands, hoping to leverage favors into great fame and become a bigger star, turn to page 9.

Breathe. Imagine freedom. Envision where the gears might be, you tell yourself while working the quill like a lock pick, concentrating. Time passes as you keep digging and twisting, hoping it doesn't snap. You can't help but think about all the struggles and strife in your life: growing up poor in small-town Wisconsin, admiring the circus as it came through town, hustling tricks, learning circus acrobatics, running away, apprenticing with a locksmith, finally earning some money for your family. You can't be held back now.

You hate feeling stuck.

Turn to the next page.

8

You tweak the feather in and out of the lock, using all your knowledge about padlocks to try to open the cell door. Nothing works. It looks like you can slip through the window if you contort your body. You are spry and very fit from years of conditioning, acrobatic training, swimming, running, and boxing. Still, you are not sure about climbing out and scaling the brick building.

Luckily, you hear a *POP!* releasing the lock of the cell door . . . but you hear approaching footsteps. *Quick, do something!*

If you choose to stop escaping and wait since someone is coming, turn to page 10.

If you choose to climb out the small window and scale the building, turn to page 20.

"It's true, I have studied locks and keys extensively. I will help you," you tell Rohan. You agree to be a do-gooder.

"Call me Big Andy!" Rohan says, pleased you will train the enforcement team in your skills. After a day of showing the police your secrets, you are bored.

"C'mon," you chide Rohan. "Is this it? Isn't there a bigger mission or something?" Rohan and the other cops grunt and agree, you've done enough. They tell you that you are free to leave. "As long as you can get out that door," they say, nodding toward a thick, padlocked grate.

Turn to the next page.

You are examining the door when an official with a mustache and an intimidating presence appears.

"Why, hello there, Mr. Houdini! How amazing to meet you. I am the Chief of the U.S. Secret Service, John E. Wilkie," he says, shutting the heavy door. "I heard you were looking for a bigger mission."

"What is the Secret Service? That sounds . . . like a secret!"

"We are a government bureau in charge of collecting national data and arresting criminals. And you know what, Sir Houdini, I am also a magician!"

"You are?" You are curious, even though you know everyone wants to be one.

"I coordinate counter-intelligence. Entertainers are great for espionage . . . you are all so bright, and such quick learners. It is very American to help. Even Abraham Lincoln recruited a magician, Horatio G. Cooke, as a scout during the Civil War."

"I didn't know that! Well, what do you need me to do?" you ask, feeling proud.

Go on to the next page.

"We need you to use your connections, position, and talents to spy on criminals, especially some major counterfeiters. These people are ruining the country. They are stealing money by copying it and swindling everyone!"

"Oh yes, I knew some of those types from my sideshow days."

"The counterfeiters are brutes—the worst! They will kidnap or hurt anyone in their way. As a magician, you already have many spy skills. You are an expert in secrecy and deception. You will also need the great art of escape in any situation. We will train you in recognizing fake silver and gold. This will be very dangerous."

"I adore danger," you assure him.

"We can help you become more famous," Wilkie tells you, "if you help us. And because I like you, I'll even give you a choice: first, you may return to the Coney Island sideshow. Catch up on new spy skills from your friends and bring them back to us. We can use their skills to take down crime in the West End—where the racing and gambling are rampant."

"Ah, I see. For instance, the lobster boy who showed me to pick locks. That might come in handy."

"You mean 'that might come in claw-y'?"

"Hahaha," you both chuckle at the same time.

Turn to the next page.

"And if I don't want to exploit my friends at Coney Island, and sell you their secrets?" you ask Wilkie. "What's my other choice?"

"Or . . . Mr. Houdini, we will book you on a tour of the Orpheum Theaters. There, we believe the manager, tycoon Martin Beck, owes a lot of money because he opened too many theaters too quickly. He's printing his own money to pay his debts. He is a suave actor, but he's not operating alone."

Now, this would be the biggest break of your career. Orpheum Theaters are the most popular places.

"This tour would bring you fame—and you would head out West into the hub of the counterfeiting rings. You would gather intelligence, so we can bust them. But just know, the counterfeiters use a mold made from a real silver dollar, and the fakes are difficult to identify," he says, holding up two coins that look absolutely identical, no matter which way he turns them.

"That is confusing! But it's great to be working together," you say, shaking his hand, happy that whatever you choose, you gain something.

Do you choose to hop onto the Orpheum Theater tour and spy as a performing observer to help the Secret Service? If so, turn to page 15.

Would you rather choose to visit the Coney Island freak show to learn better tricks in pursuit of the bad guys? If so, turn to page 28.

Come to the Orpheum for Martin **Beck**'s mystic friend ~Harry **Houdini** is the wonder of Vaudville: "The only conjurer in the world to escape handcuffs, shackles, leg cuffs, insane belts, with a sealed mouth; he carries **no** keys, springs, wires or concealed accessories!"

The Orpheum circuit boasts the most exciting entertainment in the country, and its entertainers are the best paid as well. You cannot turn down the chance to perform in the most opulent theaters across the Midwest and West. Each show has animal acts, opera, comedy, dancing, mind readers. And of course, magic.

You perform the needle-swallowing, straitjacket, card, and box tricks. As you travel and perform, you charm Martin Beck, a well-traveled, business-focused straight shooter. You eavesdrop and follow Beck's every move, winning over his friendship while collecting intel about his contacts and daily habits.

He gives you the best slot of all the times to perform, second to last. Everyone is flocking to see you, eager for you to entertain them.

"I am the Great Houdini, Master Mystifier!" you yell for your huge crowds in Cincinnati, St. Louis, Kansas City, Omaha, and Denver. No more eating out of cans and making a wild-caught rabbit last days and days rather than starving. No more rat-infested lodging.

Special posters are made announcing the Orpheum tours. An "advancer" plasters them all over each town ahead of every show to attract audiences. Everyone is told that you are such a big star that you must approve every poster. What you are really doing is hiding Wilkie's secret messages in the posters, so his other agents can see them.

Turn to the next page.

Upon each arrival of the vaudeville caravan, you awaken before dawn and add hidden messages to your show posters for the Secret Service agents. You smile at yourself, inking in the codes.

"Great job!" the singing act tells you as you walk offstage that evening. All the actors applaud you while you receive a standing ovation. You are in Cincinnati tonight, and you just dazzled everyone, making twenty-five cards disappear one by one, then making them reappear, one by one, using the back-of-the-palm trick.

You have the most desired time slot and are paid the most money. You feel terrible guilt since all of your new friends perform multiple times a day for less pay. They are forced to manage other duties like caring for the animals, hauling huge trunks at load-in, and costume-making. They are your family. More and more, the other performers, especially the children, complain about their pay. They believe Beck is lying about the show's actual income and underpaying the performers.

Each night you triumph and take many bows. But the glory feels stained. You realize: it's time to do something.

Go on to the next page.

One night in St. Louis, you pal around with Beck after the show while he counts money. He tells you outrageous stories of the Wild West, gunfights, and Buffalo Bill. His stories do not distract you from his con, and you notice he is placing handfuls of coins into a different bag. He notices you watching. "It's very expensive to run this operation, you know." He hands you a real coin for your compliance.

"Are these real?" you ask . . . and then covering up your intentions, you say: "Hey, I could use some fake money for the audience challenges. We could start offering 100 silver dollars to anyone who can keep me locked up. Now that would bring in crowds . . . "

Turn to the next page.

Beck agrees and you offer the challenge for a few weeks. Huge crowds come in and try to win. You leave poster messages about it to implicate Beck, but no arrest is made. Since no one captures him, you decide you must do it yourself to stop the rip-off. You hatch a plan: trap Beck in your box trick!

After arriving in Denver, you taunt Beck: "C'mon, try The Metamorphosis out! It's thrilling. You should know how this works. In fact, I will tell you secrets I have told no one." Beck inspects the box and you explain the trick.

"First, we will go into the audience to borrow a coat. You will put it on. You will lock me in the box, shackled with ropes. You'll lock the box and draw the curtain. Within seconds we will have switched places and you will be in the box and I will be free in the coat—much to the audience's awe. We will create suspense together!"

"Well, I certainly admire you . . . I might as well find out what the excitement is all about!" Beck says, and he agrees to be onstage with you as the assistant who will switch places with you.

*Circle all the **bold** letters to find the message hidden in the poster:*

Come to the Orpheum for Martin **Beck's** mystic fri**end** ~Harry **Houdini** is the **w**onder of Vaudville: "**T**he only conjurer in the w**o**rld to esc**ap**e **h**andcuffs, shackles, leg cuffs, **i**nsane belts, with a sealed **m**outh; he carries **no** keys, springs, **w**ires or concealed accessories**!**"

Go on to the next page.

"Ladies, and Gentleman, now The Metamorphosis, also known as The Great Trunk Mystery!" you bellow from the stage, looking out at the sea of people. Huge gas lights illuminate faces in the crowd. They're all mystified. You feel their energy pulsing through you. "Watch this box transform our bodies! I, the Great Houdini, will enter the box. I will be bound by ropes inside, have it sealed, and then magically change places with my assistant," you boast, pointing at Beck, who loves the theatrics. "All I need is a jacket from a member of the crowd!"

To add showmanship, you enter the audience to borrow a coat. You recognize Agent Rohan! He thrusts his coat at you, cramming a small paper in your hands. *I must appear flawless to the audience,* you think, and do not react, hopping back onstage. You conceal it and dip offstage to peek at it, grabbing the curtain that will hide the cabinet during the switch-over. The note says:

We got your messages
DO NOT bother Beck yet!

You should obey but maybe you don't care, you are so mad at Beck. No one scams your friends.

If you choose to stick with your plan to trap Beck in the box, turn to page 21.

Or, if you choose to remain on the circuit to California and try taking the whole counterfeit hub down, turn to page 24.

20

You squeeze your body out of the window and scale down the brick building, inhaling your freedom. You shimmy along, grabbing on to each brick as if you are a spider.

You slip, and bricks gouge you as your body bangs against the wall. You regain your footing. You are so close. Still, all you can think about is how the papers will go berserk when they learn you have escaped the famous Chicago police! You are so caught up imagining these headlines that you lose your footing once and for all.

The End

"Each time I do this trick, dear audience, I do not know what will happen!" you yell just before you drop down into the velvet bag. Beck cinches it in ropes, slams the box, and nails it shut, banging on every side then standing on top of it.

Within seconds of the curtain going up around the trunk, you climb out of the box and shimmy out of Rohan's coat, throwing it to Beck. Beck pulls the coat on and you switch places. Then you hop on top of the box just as the curtain drops again.

You see Rohan stealthily approaching from the aisles, a threatening expression on his face. You wonder if Rohan even knows about Wilkie's telegram: maybe he's here to catch Beck on his own? You aren't sure if you can trust him.

You wave your fist in an uproar of triumph. Out of the corner of your eye, you see Rohan give an usher a shove. The usher falls, knocking a huge gas lamp over. The curtains around him rapidly catch on fire.

Turn to the next page.

"Fire! Fire!" Screams overtake the theater. Everyone darts for the exit.

Before you rush out with them, you give Rohan a long stare. He must have been out to get you, but why? Was he in cahoots with Beck? Did he crack the poster message and use it to sabotage both you and the mission? Does he want the money himself?

Beck is locked in the box, and the theater is about to go up in a blaze. You need to act fast, and you don't want to lose Rohan in the chaos.

While you waver, the fire grows around you. "Lemme out!!" Beck pounds from inside the box.

You look around the theater. The fire is overtaking it faster than you would have thought possible. You may not have enough time to free Beck and save yourself.

Turn to page 80.

24

"Great frontier, here we come!" you shout as all the vaudevillians board the Overland Limited train the next day. You are bound for San Francisco to perform at the original Orpheum Theater. The trip takes a long time, and you spend it practicing tricks and mingling with the other passengers. By day you pass tallgrass prairies, majestic mountain ranges, wide-open skies, blazing sunsets, ghost towns, and peach-colored high deserts. By night, you gamble in the club car, using sleight of hand and distraction to gain big winnings.

"Oh, stop beating us!" your fellow passengers plead with you. You collect fake coins from one of the wealthier businessmen, Stasio, when you beat him. Your training in identifying faux money alerts you immediately, but you say nothing to Stasio at first. You surveille him for days, eavesdropping and befriending.

You thought you would find leads to counterfeiters in San Francisco, but maybe you are sharing the train with an actual counterfeiter now.

Turn to the next page.

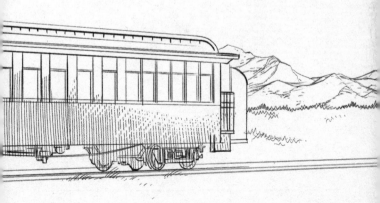

One night when you're almost in San Francisco, you gamble as the train chugs along. You overhear Stasio in the nighttime fun car boasting to a land buyer: "Ah, see these coins? They are made from metal pulled from small silver mines out near Chico," he says slyly, "and they're flooding fake money into circulation." Your ears perk up and you nearly jump across the seats. Stasio notices. You try not to let on that you're interested, switching topics by divulging vaudeville gossip. He soon gets up and leaves.

Go on to the next page.

You remind yourself that no matter what clues Stasio gives, your mission is to find the source of the counterfeiting operation, and you can't blow your cover over a few fake coins. You excuse yourself and follow Stasio down through several train cars.

You think you're being stealthy, but he looks behind and sees you. Stasio enters the next car and so do you, but then you don't see him. You keep walking, everyone around you asleep and snoring.

Suddenly you feel a hand on your shoulder and a rag is pressed to your mouth. Inhaling fumes from the cloth, you pass out.

When you wake up, you are inside a trunk. You don't know where you are, but you hear the train moving. Total darkness. You have been in many dark boxes, but you are not in control, and you're more scared than you've ever been.

Turn to page 43.

"This place is alive with energy!" you exclaim to your taxi driver with glee upon arriving at Coney Island. Its fun-filled Sea Lion Park is New York City's beach getaway. It is full of swimmers, thrills, and hot dogs galore. Steamboats and trains make visiting easy. The amusement park draws all sorts of activity: a Ferris Wheel, fancy gardens, performers, water acrobats, human anomalies, and animal acts.

Barkers yawp loudly, telling people which show to attend, trying to sell tickets:

"Come see the camel girls do the camel walk! The virtuoso Spanish guitarist with missing fingers!"

"No, no, come see our iridescent mummy. And a real mermaid!"

It's overwhelming, but eventually, you see friends from past sideshows and circus work: the giant couple, the lizard people, and the human window pane—whose heart you can see beat through his skin.

"Hi Eva!" you yell when you see dazzling Eva Thardo, Queen of Pain—she can tolerate anything. She turns around, surprised, giving her spangly costume a tug. "Harry!?!" Eva has a snake wrapped around her arm. "You're just in time. I'm going to demonstrate withstanding snake bites," she announces, heading up on stage with her long snake.

Turn to page 30.

"Oh great, I could use this practice to combat torture by snake venom," you say, and watch in amazement as Eva withstands several snake bites. When she takes her final bow, you notice tiny rivers of blood dripping down her legs.

"It's like you got into a brawl with the Cactus Boy," you joke as she joins you off stage.

"Ha! Come with me," Eva says. "You must meet The Professor. Her job is to introduce each freak to the audience and tell tall tales of their origins and abilities. She knows everything!" Eva introduces you and you trust her immediately. You admire teachers. You tell her why you are there, to investigate and gain skills from the outcasts.

Go on to the next page.

"I will introduce you to everyone!" The Professor promises. "Here, look at this, Harry," she says, holding the embryologist's egg glass up to a sealed envelope. You peer through it and can read the writing on the letter inside.

You press her for secrets that stump you. "But tell me, how did Eva survive her snakebite trick?"

"She drinks milk, only milk," The Professor confides.

Turn to the next page.

32

The Professor leads you to The Strongman Fish and Cora the Contortionist, who often perform together.

"Say, guys, can you show me any escape tricks? I, uh, need it for my next . . . act." You don't share your reasons, but it's not exactly a lie—you long to take your act on the road again.

They love showing off, so they don't mind sharing their secrets.

"Here's how to puff up your body." Strongman Fish expands his muscles while Cora ties him up with ropes. Once the ropes are tied, Fish unclenches his muscles to create enough slack to escape. You practice chest expansions. Cora demonstrates how to adjust your shoulders out of place and pop them back into their sockets, in case you ever need to escape from ropes.

And then The Armless Wonder shows up. He does all his tricks with his feet.

"Here's how to manipulate your toes in case you are ever tied up and need to write a message."

"Or pick locks with my feet—brilliant!" you say.

"Ahh, of course. Isn't it great here? No one makes fun of my limbs in this world," he says, reminding you of how accepting performers are because no one is "normal." You are so happy to be in an accepting place.

Go on to the next page.

You spend days and days absorbing the knowledge. You feel as if you are gaining superpowers. Who should you visit next? You look around at the stages for The Swift Sword Swallowers, The Dangerous Kazim, The Dog-Faced Boy, and The Tattooed Cat Woman. All of them sound exciting, and all of them could teach you tricks.

Do you decide to study regurgitation with The Swift Sword Swallowers? Turn to the next page.

If you want to visit The Dangerous Kazim to learn how to dematerialize, turn to page 36.

If you wish to find The Dog-Faced Boy, turn to page 44.

Or shall you find The Tattooed Cat Woman, who knows inks and codes? If so, turn to page 94.

The Swift Sword Swallowers are a very important act. They demonstrate high-risk skills you could adapt, like how to swallow picks and keys to regurgitate when needed. You watch them again and again, barely able to stomach it.

But you do also love the shock value. Blade after blade, swords slide down their throats into their bellies. It doesn't seem to bother them if they nick their mouth or esophagus! But how?

Turn to page 39.

36

"Welcome, what doth thee need to know?" The Dangerous Kazim asks you as you approach his simple stage lit by a single, thick candle. He looks very mystical, from another time and place. You tell him you are interested in learning the secrets of his tricks. He thinks this over.

"You must give me your blood, a poem, and a lock of your hair."

"Umm, okay," you tell him. You slice off some hair using your pocket tool and offer your finger for a prick. You make up a poem on the spot, exaggerating your powers:

> *I come from an immigrant life of struggle and strife,*
> *That makes me so real, so strong I will not abide*
> *By any rules that restrain me.*
> *Unless, of course, they are the Laws of Spirit—*
> *Through which the gods help me break free; for all to fear it!*

Go on to the next page.

Then, The Dangerous Kazim grabs the blood and steps into the ghost cabinet. "This is my vehicle, I'm off to another world," he says as he closes the door.

"Ohhh," you answer, looking the cabinet over. You know a lot about cabinets from your show . . . often there is a fake wall and hiding places for things.

You wait for him to speak from inside or emerge. You fling open the door, but he's gone! Did he really dissolve out of his body?

Turn to page 39.

Your mind buzzing with questions, you hear the most beautiful melodies from another stage. Songs that draw you to them, enchanted, songs that sound like birds singing. You follow the music until you enter the show tent marked "Bess-the-Bird and the Floral Sisters."

Angelic singers adorned in flowers dance and sing on stage, soothing you with their chorus. The lead, Bess, is in a feathery costume. She even looks naturally lithe and bird-like—she can fit easily into any box.

You approach her after the performance. "Miss Bess, wait. I'm Harry Houdini. You were magnificent, totally inspiring. I feel like a bird, one who can go anywhere, do anything! We should team up and flock together."

"Team up? But I have my sisters, we blossom song in others . . . I mean . . . "

"That is beautiful, but eventually the act will bore you. I promise excitement, near-death-defying feats that extend beyond the material world."

You are mesmerized by Bess, and you have a deep conversation. You can't help but tell her you are a special agent, and if you agree to join forces, she must become one as well. "If you wish, you can sing the famous circus songbook on the road. I myself am a master of marvels and reign as the Wizard of Shackles."

"Oh, my. This is getting stale, same songs night after night. Let's fly toward greatness together!"

Turn to the next page.

Then, just as you leave for the causeway, The Dangerous Kazim materializes before you. It seems like a sea of stars shines down on his ruby velvet cape. His hair is electric and curly and silver as the moon. You reach out to hug him, and he vanishes entirely. There is so much magic here on Coney Island.

Totally mesmerized from the days' events, you realize you forgot to report back to Wilkie and the Secret Service. While Wilkie may one day make you an American hero, you miss the magic, adventure, and the open road before you had a boss to report to.

That evening, you take a walk on the beach at Old Iron Pier to think about Coney Island, Wilkie, and your future. A slate-gray sky collects clouds that cluster into a huge, malevolent storm.

The beach hosts water shows and aquatic inventions, as well as large sculptures and curios scattered across it, and you come upon a huge ball of yarn. *A giant toy,* you think as you start to unravel it. Your mind unravels as you unravel the yarn. *Slip a stitch . . . hmmm . . . time to switch paths, create something new.*

Suddenly, the yarn's other end starts moving. As you turn to look, it lassos your feet. You are caught and tugged down, face-planting into the sand!

Go on to the next page.

"We are onto you! We know who you are working for and we will do away with you," two voices say, as rough hands pull you up. It's The Professor and The Strongman Fish! They shove you onto the carousel. You bob up and down on an extravagantly painted mermaid.

The Professor glides beside you on a painted horse.

"You're reporting to the Secret Service! You're helping them, and you're looking for counterfeiters," she says. How could she know? But then you remember—she's The Professor. She sees, and knows, everything.

"Why are you so concerned? Do you two know any counterfeiters?"

Turn to the next page.

"Maybe we do," says Fish. "We got into some trouble gambling. Why don't you join forces with us? You can help us fix the cards. We will cut you half of our half of the winnings."

You think about it.

"Say, if we work it right, you'll be able to afford yourself a nice home in New York City," suggests The Professor.

"A house!" Your dream is to move your mother and siblings into a family house, and you've loved being here at Coney Island. The offer is tempting. And you don't want to be exposed if you say no. The "freaks" already do not trust many outsiders, and they will shun you as exploiting them if they find out who you work for. You think about Bess, and also about your original assignment.

If you decide to distract them so you can leave immediately with Bess and launch your own improved act, turn to page 45.

If you agree to the opportunity to abort the original mission and become a rich criminal, turn to page 121.

If you choose to go report to Wilkie, turn to page 52.

"Hey! Help!" you yell, but your voice is overwhelmed by the *choo-choo* and the rhythms of the train on the tracks. You are still on the same train headed West, at least, but you assume you're in the luggage boxcar where no one can help you. You figure you can escape . . . if you don't panic.

You have enough room to move around, but as you do, you realize you aren't alone in the trunk. Something big skitters along the inside of the trunk's lid, brushing your face. You panic, but remember certain bugs live in wooden trunks and the most common one out West is the crab-pincer—which has gargantuan claws—that you could use! Intercepting it as it scurries across your chest, you smash it between your fingers, jerk the pincers out, and begin cramming them into the lock. Angling it properly, you push open the top just a bit, careful not to show your face in case the person who captured you is still nearby. It's dawn and the sky is becoming pink when you see early shafts of light. A hobo sleeps on luggage nearby and he looks incredibly mean.

The hard part will be staying safe once you are outside this box of death.

If you decide to close the trunk and wait inside until you reach the station, turn to page 84.

Do you bust out and hope for the best, maybe even revenge? If so, turn to page 114.

When you meet The Dog-Faced Boy, Fedor, you are taken aback. He wears a Russian pink army suit, with silken hair spilling down his face, parted in the middle. He looks just like a dog! Is it real? Will he bark?

He reads your fear and barks at you. "Everyone expects me to bark, but I actually speak Russian, German, and English."

"Me too!" You smile at your connection. Fedor studies you.

"I deceive by what others misperceive." He gives you tips on misdirection, how to distract onlookers. You learn how attention works. "While they are staring at me in disgust or confusion, I *woof* like they expect me to but then I crawl around pickpocketing," he says. "Everyone thinks that a hunter found me and my dad and captured us. P. T. Barnum called us savages who could not be civilized."

"That is so mean!"

You pull your hair down over your face, which you often also part down the middle.

"Say, I've been called a hungry wolf before. Let me be your brother, and we can have an act!" The two of you lock arms and play wild animals wrestling. A beautiful friendship begins.

The End

"C'mon, join us, we know you have magic powers you can harness for cash!" Fish urges.

You decide to fake them out: "I will show you how to fix cards, and how to set them up for the big clean-up. Let's discuss this further . . . over there, on the Flip-Flap Railway," you suggest, pointing to the brand-new roller coaster.

You all climb into the car for the ride. The roller coaster is swooping, rickety, and rough. As the car *click-click-clicks* along the track, you know you can hypnotize them if you speak soothingly.

"Money money money," you murmur as their eyes slowly shut, just before the coaster's big dip.

You leap off the ride and land on the ground.

Turn to page 97.

46

"Europe will surely make me famous or a hero!" you announce with pride and bravado, confident that either way, you are bound for major stardom. You board the *SS Kensington* to travel across the Atlantic Ocean to Great Britain. You were given no contacts for the tour or information for your next task. Soon you are performing for important people and sailors on board.

But you become very, very seasick. For such a strong, steadfast person, no one can believe how woozy and incapacitated you are.

Turn to page 48.

48

"Superman, what's your plan upon arrival?" the sailors jab at you, visiting you in the infirmary. When you aren't totally delirious, you manage to tell them the name of the hotel and performance hall: the Atlantean. One of them informs you there is no theater—and definitely no hotel—there anymore. You're confounded, and feel like throwing yourself overboard . . . but of course, you are always resilient.

Maybe this isn't so bad. I am not sure about the spy path anyway, you think. While it might be rewarding, it has been constricting to your creativity.

You arrive in a dismal, gray London. You are haggard, and you limp along, looking for food and a boarding house to stay in. You finally find an affordable one at 10 Keppel Street and pass out.

Go on to the next page.

You recoup your energy and your land legs, and you begin banging on theater doors to audition. "Stupendous! Majestic! A marvel of a man!" are the headlines from your scrapbook of newspaper praise from America that you haul around with you to shove in front of agents.

This should be no problem, you assure yourself, as you audition all around London. You cross the cobbled, curving streets of the theater district, clenching your fists with stress as your funds dwindle. Yet you conjure up a carefree air to appeal as an entertainer. You audition and audition, but nothing seems to stick. You're puzzled. Londoners patronize music halls, but the cuff game has been around a while, dominated by a chap called The Great Cirnoc.

Repeatedly, you visit the Alhambra Theatre, a popular variety theater, begging for a shot. Finally, a talent agent there named Slater tells you to challenge Scotland Yard. "It will make you stand out. Especially if you can get past the head of foreign intelligence."

Even though you are nervous, of course, you should challenge the most famous police force of all time. You take a carriage ride over to the massive station and campus and insist on being brought to the chief.

Turn to page 51.

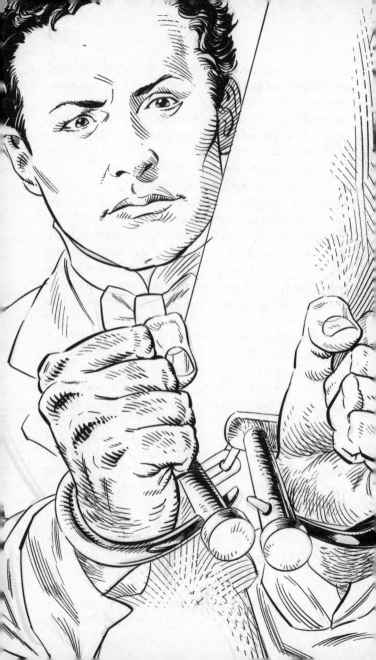

"Nice to meet you, Harry, I am Sir William Melville. I am the head of Scotland Yard's special branch of intelligence for Great Britain . . . . Actually, I work for Agent Wilkie from America. We have been waiting for you."

"What—Wilkie? I haven't heard a peep from him since I left! He lied to me!"

"We were testing you. We still are."

Melville signals to his men, and they handcuff you in Darby cuffs—the very best irons—around a marble column. Luckily, you know how to escape these specific cuffs by banging them at the right spot. You only have one shot; if you bang it incorrectly, you could jam the lock forever.

"Say, if I get out of these, can you call up your friend Slater at the Alhambra and get me booked?"

"If you get out of these, I'll help you with whatever—but you will have to help *us* more!" he guffaws.

You suspect your accuracy is off after your seasickness and dreary trip. Maybe you should try to wiggle free instead?

If you trust that you know exactly where to slam the cuffs, even though your accuracy is off from being seasick, turn to page 53.

If you decide to wiggle your hands out of the cuffs, turn to page 85.

"You have done the most excellent work!" Wilkie informs you upon your return. The Secret Service believes you could be an expert spy. "We will send you to Europe where you can build world recognition," Wilkie tells you.

"But I have just started rising like a meteor to the top performer here!" you protest.

"Yes, but we need you to go abroad to England to meet with Inspector William Melville. You have more important work to do. Very, very important work. Work that could save the whole world. We will send you first class across the Atlantic on a grand ocean liner, and an assistant will wait on you. You will live in luxury and be very noble."

Shouldn't you stay in America where you are already a celebrity?

Do you leave America in hopes of world recognition? If so, turn to page 46.

Or do you stay in America, where you are already famous? If so, turn to page 81.

In one fell swoop, you slam the cuffs and free yourself with lightning speed. Luck is on your side. "Hey wait, I will join you for lunch—on you!" you shout and laugh, shucking the cuffs off. They are all stunned and humbled. They have no choice but to take you out.

After the meal, Melville says, "We need you to help us . . . with spying. Name your price."

"To be booked at the majestic Alhambra Theatre," you insist. Melville agrees, if you'll complete a mission for him.

Melville gives you a fancy room at Scotland Yard and teaches you about contraptions and spy skills: how to heat-seal letters, to handle a spy dart umbrella and a periscope mirror that can be placed on a hat that will help you look behind you or backward or around a corner. You teach him a few tricks, too.

Together, you practice the best techniques in eavesdropping, reading lips, and how to transmit information through telegrams, publications, and . . . your hair!

Turn to the next page.

54

"I am free of your fetters!" you boast from inside the regal, multicolored rotunda of Alhambra Theatre of Variety as you escape yet again. You feel your voice travel out to the promenade, past the facade, the fancy twin minarets, beyond the fountain, throughout Leicester Square in the West End. Each night you challenge different members of the press who bring shackles as well as high-tech makers, welders, and manufacturers to bind you with whatever iron they create. You wear your fanciest black frock coat with a pristine white bowtie and a chin-high collar to perform. You dress to impress, hoping the Queen will attend.

Sandwich boards advertise you: "World's Greatest Mystifier! Master of Manacles!" You share the stage with whirling dervishes, Saharet the dancer, clog dancers clopping, and ballerinas. There is even animatography on a movie projector. Guests sing along to musical acts, drinking and eating their cares away. You feel glamorous and unstoppable.

Turn to page 56.

One night, Slater informs you: "The Queen of England is coming tonight. I want you to challenge one of our own performers, for extra excitement and press coverage."

"Of course! I shall give my best showmanship. Hmmm . . . how about Magnetic Girl? She is the most popular and confounding. Metal in my cuffs will eliminate her electricity." You've watched Georgia Magnet, night after night, known for her superhuman strength, able to use her own magnetism to control the force of gravity. Even though she stands on a Tesla coil mat that kept her "insulated" from the ground, you do not believe she simply increases her weight and becomes so heavy that no one can lift or even faze her.

"No man can force me from my mat, no matter the number of attempts. I have a force from the spirits!" she announces to you onstage.

"But I am supernatural! I am superman! I can release her from the grip of the spirits," you charge, and wrap every type of metal cuff around her, trying to stop the electricity, but her trick is better than yours and you do not succeed. You see the Queen in the audience. And Melville. Afterward, only Melville comes back to the dressing room. There are no royal congratulations.

Go on to the next page.

"Houdini, we have a mission to collect intel to help us avert a major World War. I am sending you to Germany, where we believe Kaiser Wilhelm II, the King of Prussia, is building an empire to overtake us—and America! He desires total world power. He's already increased the power of the German navy. Wilhelm is obsessed with huge ships, and inventions, just like you. But you are controlled, and he is very impulsive."

"Hmmm . . . interesting. I speak German! But I am on top of my game here."

"Are you, though? After tonight?" He chuckles. "Well, I'll sweeten the deal. You can even bring your brother, The Great Hardeen!"

"We call him Dash . . . or Theo."

"Ha. Yes, well, have Dash dash on over. Tell him the apples are ripe! We already know he is a magician himself and that might help the ruse. But he must be vetted and trained as well. Afterward, in exchange, we will give you new passports that let you travel anywhere and claim your own homelands. Won't you like that?"

Turn to the next page.

58

"Yes, but what about magic?"

"There will be plenty! Your reputation as Houdini hinges on the ability to use distraction and charm as your show routine! We don't mean to change that at all. It is already natural for you to carry a large number of odd items, including lock-picking tools! See, you are the perfect nomad agent to relay from abroad—traveling for work and mingling with many important people you will never be suspected." Melville smiles at you, certain he's got you now.

"Send back information on whatever you see, hear, or observe. Especially any talk of invasions, targets, their artillery, and development of aircraft. It's important to do your best to avoid writing to me directly—destroy anything written down. To communicate from a distance, you may publish encoded messages. Slip them into your reporting for the *Conjurer's Journal*."

"What if I don't go?" Unsure of denying Melville, the highest-profile police officer in England, you tread lightly.

"Well, you'd be stuck on this island and lose your shot at fame. And I'd say, after tonight, you might be drowning." He chuckles, knowing you love fame too much.

If you accept Melville's offer and become a spy in Germany, turn to page 63.

If you decline and stick with your act, turn to page 117.

You rejoin the performers and begin your performances at the Orpheum. After a while, you have a break from performing and are eager to explore San Francisco. The city is a hothouse of people doing their own thing. Spiritualists, Victorian gadabouts, and entrepreneurs starting new businesses walk amongst each other. But you learn nothing new about counterfeiting operations.

"This place is amazing," you say as you take the streetcar around the hilly city, visiting a bustling shipping center, new hotels, Golden Gate Park, the ocean, and North Beach.

You immerse yourself in the new land. You meet other magicians. You talk to other people about Spiritualism, a belief that spirits can contact the living world. "You see, there is an infinite intelligence that governs the world, and we can tap into it," the fortune-teller you share the stage with tells you.

Your performer friends offer to take you to what is called a "medium." A medium contacts the other world and summons ghosts for messages and visits to the living.

If the medium is so powerful, maybe they can help me find out more about the counterfeiters, you think. Your friends tell you about a famous psychic woman, Mystic O, who can facilitate apparitions and make ghosts materialize. She even speaks in tongues.

Turn to the next page.

60

"Yes, introduce me to Mystic O," you agree. You have always been intrigued by the afterlife, by what happens after death. You enter the psychic's large Victorian house. It is painted lavender and plum, quite a "Painted Lady." You join dinner in the library, with the gramophone playing. Mystic O lifts the needle, abruptly ending the music.

Nine people are with you, chosen by their status and name and number to appease the spirits. "Come to the circle," Mystic O says, motioning for you all to hold hands. "They can guide from beyond the grave."

You are not sure about this.

"Now we call in the energies," Mystic O announces soothingly. Everyone stares into the dark and hears a muffled trumpet sound. "My spirit guides have arrived . . . they will relay any messages from the dead to us. Who would like to go first?"

"I will. What messages are there for me, the Great Mystifying Houdini?" you boast, not really believing in this kind of magic. You know everything is a show for entertainment.

Turn to page 62.

62

The medium loses herself in trance. "Ohhh," Mystic O moans, then begins speaking in tongues. You hear a knocking sound. She says someone is coming in from the afterlife. But you know there is likely a tapping mechanism connected to her toes.

You remain suspicious when, suddenly, a small skeleton appears, striding toward you bending its knees and elbows. Several red rosebuds appear as well, and together they swirl around in the air. You have been told any manifestation of objects is a gift from the spirit world, but you cannot believe what you see fly in the air!

"Why, we are all just skeletons and love, after all!" you scoff, pulling down a rose.

The table begins shaking. It levitates, rising just a bit and then lifting three feet into the air. A gauzy, diaphanous blob of see-through whiteness forms over the medium's head.

"Ectoplasm," the man seated next to you explains.

"Ah, your father is here," says Mystic O.

"What? How would you know?"

"He was a rabbi named Mayer Samuel," she states with vigor. You told no one that! Do you continue or do you decide to stop this silly seance?

If you agree to continue talking to your dead father, turn to page 75.

Or if you think this is ridiculous and try to debunk the seance, turn to page 110.

"I'll go!" you agree. "I do so love—and conquer—every adventure. But I also demand you make my immediate wish come true."

"Oh? What is that?"

"For me to perform at London's new Hippodrome, while we train."

Melville agrees. You spend another month in London performing in front of thousands of people. You feel even more powerful amidst grand marble columns, lush velvet carpeting, oak floors, a full circus hall, and a huge gallon tank for water acts. Thousands of people fill the theater—thousands! Though you are a box office hit, you must stay true to your word.

You train further in surveillance and eaves-dropping with Melville. Inventing and fabricating are your favorite things to do, so together you work on black felt disguises, periscopes, and poison resistance.

Turn to the next page.

64

"*Guten tag*, Germany!" you yell from your train as you arrive. You are very ready for the thrills of a new country. You tour immediately, and perform a rigorous schedule: Berlin, Munich, Dresden, Hanover, and on and on. Soon you are adored for your showmanship. It also helps that you speak German, which you learned in childhood.

Eavesdropping, you pick up information as you mingle with important people, military even, who share and boast about increased militarization of cars, aircraft development, and naval dominance.

"Yes, Essen!" You land in an industrial Essen for a three-week run of shows. You are eager to perform there, as it is the home of Krupp munitions—a massive manufacturer of warcraft. If you can get into the factory, surely you can glean intel to report to Melville. As soon as you step off the train, you are greeted by the young head of the factory.

"I am Bertha Krupp, your host and the heir of the company. I hereby challenge you to these special, foolproof cuffs designed by our great Krupp Factory!" She nearly spits on you, looming over you as you stare at industrial-strength, iron handcuffs. The escape is sure to be grueling, even hurtful.

You play it cool, confident. "If I win, I shall be allowed to visit the munitions factory."

Turn to page 66.

66

"Oh? If you would like to see our famous, top-secret factory, we will have to up the stakes." Fräulein Krupp sounds threatening.

"Fine," you bargain. "As long as Hardeen is my assistant."

That night, people travel from all over the region for the challenge, including the press. "Welcome to my very special show—presenting the Mania Cuffs! I am Herr Houdini, the Master of Metals, I flick off all fetters! I accept this challenge . . . I trust the cuffs are not jammed?"

"These were built by a mechanic of the highest order! However, now truly, if you are a master, you will allow us to put you in a dynamic position." Fräulein Krupp motions for you to lie on your stomach.

You question it, unsure, but play along. You know you can handle normal mania. Fräulein Krupp takes two sets of cuffs. "I shall now lock behind his back. Lie down." She twists your hands behind your back and thrusts your feet up, so you feel like a wheelbarrow, binding you in heavy leg irons. "We have challenged Houdini to win a visit to our factory. He is welcome if he can free himself!" The audience's anticipation is noticeable.

It takes many minutes to lock the screws that squeeze your wrists. Fräulein Krupp screws the cuffs down until metal touches your bone.

Go on to the next page.

You are lifted into your cabinet. Many minutes pass. "I won't give up," you repeat to yourself, "but this is torture," you admit to no one as you writhe and squirm.

The orchestra plays on, carefully choosing something to excite or calm the audience. "Please, can someone bring me a cushion!" you finally yell from inside the cabinet. They open it up to reveal that you are on your side, extremely tired but jerking around. "My hands and legs are terribly numb! Please cushion me!"

They allow your brother, Hardeen, to bring a cushion and close the cabinet. They should have hidden a key in the seam, but alas, there is none. The orchestra plays tense time signatures. At any moment your whole reputation could be ruined. Drained of blood, your limbs begin to tingle. "I believe these locks have been jammed, everyone, please be patient," you beg.

"No, they are just the finest. Our main blacksmith took years to craft these . . . The Germans make everything better!" Fräulein Krupp retorts.

Wincing in pain, you plead: "Please, can we take them off so that blood can return to my wrists and body? This is just cruelty in chains. I just need—."

"If you cannot do it, give up!" Fräulein Krupp insists. You refuse to relent and breathe into the pain.

Turn to the next page.

"Please, bring me water, my brother." You gasp, feeling half-dead. They allow him to approach the cabinet. The crowd gasps at the sight of you and cheers when you take long, dramatic sips of water.

Inside the cup is a key. You almost swallow it, but spit it out and bite it between your teeth. Then you are able to pull your legs over your head and unwind your arms so the cuffs can be unlocked.

You are free but wait for another fifty minutes in the cabinet, wishing you had a newspaper. The audience is in hysterics, not knowing if you are okay. The orchestra plays on. Finally, you emerge from the cabinet, half-dead, swollen, and discolored. So hideous are your beaten-up arms, they are still blue. You show everyone your torn skin.

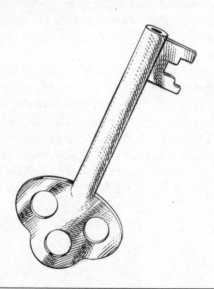

Go on to the next page.

"I apologize, ladies and gents, to show you these wounds of cruelty. The cuffs were rigged—I was set up."

The papers report endlessly about it. The next day, you visit the Krupps' Factory and are treated like a king. You are even presented with a trophy in the shape of a silver bowl with handles. "This is called a Loving Cup, they say, for those we adore!"

It is gorgeous and glimmering. You can barely hold it, your wrists are so weak.

Turn to the next page.

70

The factory is scary. The air is filled with the sounds of the repetitive motion of people's work. Bullet after bullet, weapon parts are churned out. People work like ants. It all seems so unnecessary. While Bertha Krupp shows you around, you try to act like you are in awe. You thank her like a gentleman. In your mind, you record every detail and read into every word heard. It is time to send messages back to Melville about the advancement of their weapon arsenal. You could send them by carrier pigeon, which is fast but risky. Or you could bury the information in a secret message inside a publication, and hope he's waiting for it.

If you decide to send Melville your findings by carrier pigeon, turn to page 72.

Or, if you choose to send this intel back through a secret message in a publication, turn to page 76.

You hustle your magician friends in Berlin for a pigeon. Finally, you find a trained one and endow it with magic so it becomes an extraordinary carrier pigeon that can take your documents across the continent.

You return to tour. You are frustrated by a growing number of imitators. You used to enjoy healthy competition, but now impersonators pretend to be you, and if the crowds believe them, it tarnishes your image. But you are the freest, and you make people believe deeply in getting free.

Go on to the next page.

"Call me Bond Breaker!" you yell at the crowd, night after night, performing a rigorous schedule.

"I see hundreds billed as 'World's Greatest Handcuff King,'" you say onstage. "Apparently, all you have to do in Germany to become a 'breaker' is to buy a handcuff with two keys and you are made . . . then you to steal your name or change their name to sound like mine—"

"No!" shouts a man from the audience. "YOU ARE A FRAUD!"

"You are not even American, nor have you ever broken free of—" another voice in the audience continues.

"Not true! Who are you?" you interrupt, looking out, staring at the glare of the theater lights that blind you.

"Why, I am the Great Harry Hood-ini," the imposter states as he approaches. He wears a robe and hood.

Fearing you will lose your audience to him, you retort: "Bwah! Show your face. I am the 'original' king of handcuff escapes! I am the best, you bloke! Come up here and attempt to beat me!"

As the hooded threat comes onstage, you have your assistant bring out a heavy metal rectangle with smoothed edges and two circles. "Try these famous American-made handcuffs—the infamous Bean Giant! First, I shall escape them. Then, I challenge you to do the same. I offer $500 if you succeed!"

Turn to the next page.

He can't undo them. You feel so good. Failing, Harry Hood-ini retreats back, hiding under his hood.

"You are right, Houdini, you are the best . . . my name is just Sir Paul Cirnoc, after all." And with that, Harry Hood-ini runs out as the lights go out, vanishing from magic history.

The newspapers publish accounts raving about the dramatic confrontation. "Cirnoc fails!" "The Handcuff King IS Houdini!" "Houdini defeats Harry Hood-ini!"

Crowds storm the theater. Cheers roar like thunder. But more and more imposters show up: BlueGenie, Blondini, and Hardeen, your brother. A sibling rivalry begins in theaters just across the street from each other. At first, it's good for business. You dominate the tricks and build your own brand.

You even write down your tricks so he can duplicate them, under strict rules he can't reveal them. You want to patent them and work to stop others from copying.

One night you find out your brother shared the secrets of your most popular trick . . . The Milk Crate Escape. With the public! In the magician's circle of honor, to do so is high treason!

Should you seek revenge? Or . . . instead, expose secrets in a publication to get ahead of imitators?

If you want to call your brother out for what he has done, turn to page 104.

If you want to leave your brother be and focus on stopping the other copycats, turn to page 116.

You sit tight at the table, curious and shocked.

"Your father is talking through us," the medium says. "There is only one main message from him."

"Oh, really? Tell him I already take care of mother, as was his dying wish."

"Well, he is instructing you to 'Get a REAL JOB'!"

If you agree with your father that your life is too abnormal, turn to page 120.

If you disagree with your father and stay committed to the magic game, turn to page 96.

Once you are in your dressing room, you quickly record every single detail about the factory. You write everything down, figuring you will encode it later. The press shows up to interview you, so you stash your notes into the silver loving cup and put flowers on top. When you come back, Fräulein Krupp is there with your notes in hand. She towers over you, with a mad look on her face.

"Oh, hello Fräulein."

"I was coming to congratulate you in person . . . but . . . who are these for?"

"No one. I am just a meticulous writer." You try to charm her, but you know you have been caught.

"This is treason! I knew you were a spy, Houdini. I have discussed with the top generals how WE need you to spy for Germany—in Russia. We need to know what the Russian superpower is up to. If you don't agree, I'll show you manacles that you will never escape."

You look at your banged-up body and know you have no choice but to accept the trip to Russia.

Go on to the next page.

Russia is a massive country, larger than the imagination. It is experiencing a boom of industry, undergoing increased building of factories and railways. Ruled by the Romanovs—Czar Nicholas and his wife, Czarina Alexandra—it is full of resources but also dangers.

You finally arrive in towering Moscow. It was extremely difficult to get in. You do not mention that you are Jewish. There are laws that stop Jewish people from entering Moscow's theaters. The Russian police handled you roughly—shaking you down and grilling you about your trunk of tools. You have to play up the fact that you are a magician, that your "burglar" tools are simply for entertaining. When searching your trunk, they threaten to send you back.

"I am in charge here—I am Lebedoff—do not disobey me," he growls.

"I am but a mere human man. I am here to entertain people on behalf of the Royals."

"Oh yes, Czar Nicholas loves curiosities. You may have permission." Lebedoff lets you through.

Turn to the next page.

78

You perform in Moscow's unique theaters and dinner events and wow your audiences. You discover that there is a constant police presence. It is disruptive to your well-being, even though you are so used to mingling with police. You are sure you are always being spied on, even though you are the one spying. It's hard to even think of gaining fame for your performances or spying for Melville or for the Germans. You think only of finding a way home.

The popularity of your act gains you approval from the royalty for an outdoor escape from Moscow's Butyrskaya Prison. It is all stone and intimidating, but you succeed. Your efforts don't make friends of Lebedoff and the other police, who challenge you and watch you with suspicion.

"Try our transport cell, called a *carette*," Lebedoff says, pointing to a black carriage. It is a jail-on-wheels that prisoners spend weeks in as they are transported to far-off, scary Siberia, a no-man's-land for a lifetime of exile.

Go on to the next page.

"Fine, if you allow me to communicate my success back to my brother in Germany, since your newspapers have not reported on any of my work." That comment irks them and so, after you are locked inside, you hear the wagon being wrapped in chains. "That's not fair, that's not our agreement! All I wanted is the press I deserve!" you denounce loudly, but the police act as if they can't hear you. You bang on the wall, feeling desperate.

You can attempt to escape either through the locked grate door . . . or through its floor, which is made of zinc. Luckily, you have three tools hidden on you. Inside your stomach is a metal cutter that you swallowed earlier. There is also the arm extender and key sealed in wax under your foot. What do you use to escape?

If you attempt to cut through the metal floor of the wagon, turn to page 109.

If you decide to shunt the key out the door, and angle it to unlock it, turn to page 83.

80

You're not afraid of death. You've always defied it. You've shared the stage with many people who bring the audiences messages from the dead. Several of the spiritualists even say it is possible to have a good time when dead, that you can evolve from the other side . . . or maybe even come back from the dead!

Perhaps there is time to release Beck and still survive. Deathly heat and fumes surround you. You start coughing violently. You glance around and see that the theater office is fairly clear of smoke and flame, protected by its cinder block walls. It has a balcony to the outside that you could escape from.

You may even be able to complete your mission for Wilkie if you do this. Beck's book of contacts and his tally of all of his finances are sitting on the desk in that office.

If you choose to open up the box to release Beck, turn to page 130.

If you grab Beck's book and run instead, turn to page 92.

You deny the mission, and Wilkie lets you go, on one condition: that you agree to help should the United States have to enter into a world war. Indeed, years later, you assist the U.S. Army to learn escapes in case anyone is captured during World War I. While the work is important, you never light up a stage again.

The End

You worry that if you tamper with the floor, they may really punish you. Plus it just seems impossible. You know the lock outside is just below the small window that is divided by iron bars.

First, you reach under your false heel and grab the tool to extend the pick. As you grapple with the lock, you hear the police chuckling in between snarls of angry Russian. However, you persevere, dripping in perspiration.

Before you know it, the police drop the curtain around the vehicle, so you quickly retract your key contraption. Then you hear horses being attached to the wagon.

Great, the jig must be up! They will surely let me out—to go back to the Czar's palace, you tell yourself until minutes of moving in the wagon turn into hours into days into weeks. Siberia welcomes you with stark nothingness.

The End

84

You decide to wait it out in the trunk. Upon arrival in San Francisco, you stay rigid, hiding while all the cargo is unloaded. When the dockworkers are distracted, you slip out unnoticed and dash away from the train station, making sure Stasio and his men do not follow. You find the police station and immediately telegram Wilkie. The police protect you and you stay in hiding to cool down the trail. Wilkie's agents arrive and you tell them all you know.

Turn to page 59.

You attempt to contort your wrists and wiggle out of the cuffs. You fail, and soon Melville and even his officers leave you alone out of boredom. You decide to cut into your skin with the tiny knife you have stashed in your cheek. Lowering your mouth to the column, you move the tool in between your teeth so you can saw away at the skin. You begin sweating, which is so common when you are performing.

Your wound soon pulses with life and bacteria. By the time you return to your boarding house, you are feverish. Still, you refuse to go to a doctor because you insist you must keep auditioning. You wrap your wrists well, but each time you do a cuff trick, shocking pain radiates up your arms and down to your fingers. The wrist where you gouged them turns purple, then black.

A massive, oozing infection takes over. You die without cracking a big European break.

The End

You shake and shake, transitioning out of your body. Memories and dreams flash around you as a series of images.

But when you settle, you don't feel your body and find yourself in what you can only describe as "in-between lives."

In a web of whiteness, you explore for who knows how long. It's true, you are dead, or are you? You feel so very alive. Do you finally have the freedom you are seeking?

You roam around, with no idea what to do, when a clear, white tunnel of light leads you into swirls, as if you are doing circles around the sun.

As you enter the total purity, iridescent pastel rainbows turn into ladders, and then morph into a snowfall of pearls. The shapes start glitching—switching to a dark blue blur.

Turn to the next page.

When you can finally see again, you are in a field surrounded by famous dead people. You notice the beguiling Cleopatra first, then a group of poets and artists you admire: the great American poet of the people and nature who was a nurse in the Civil War, Walt Whitman; Emma Lazarus, who wrote the poem on the Statue of Liberty; the Ancient Greek poet Sappho; and the painter Vincent Van Gogh. These luminaries are all rhyming and sharing wonderful ideas. It's fascinating, but they don't really include you.

Soon a chorus of people appears, as if out of nowhere. "Oh hey, Harry! No way. What are you doing here?" They are all people from your own career: The Fox Sisters, who first "talked to spirits," P. T. Barnum, who created the circus, and Madame Blavatsky, a self-taught religious philosopher.

"I don't really know." Though you know they are controversial to the study of magical acts, their attention thrills you.

"Maybe you can help us make contact! We have tried to communicate through so many modes, like our slate message boards we swore by when we were on the other side," the Fox Sisters are embarrassed to tell you.

You learn that both groups are trying to connect to the living for fun, for curiosity, and for help only the human world can offer.

Turn to page 90.

"I see, you are a premier ghost club—celebrity members only—for life!" you laugh.

"But so far, we can never unlock the secret to penetrating the earth world, the land I miss and yawp about!" Walt Whitman shouts. Sappho starts singing a song about yearning for the other world, but only fragments of it come out.

"With my help we can figure out how to bust through to the earth side—this is my ultimate magic trick. I know, since we have all the time in the world," you chuckle. "We can try every Halloween . . . for my fans will be holding seances."

"Emma, I love your poem on the Statue of Liberty. It was very moving to read when I came to America. And Vincent, your paintings are like a dream."

Van Gogh says, "What?" cupping his face where his cut-off ear was.

"One problem," Madame Blavatsky insists, "is that one has to know what object they will use to summon you. This is the only way to create a proper signal. I am not making this part up! Houdini, do you know what they will use to summon you?" she asks.

Go on to the next page.

"Either a . . . um . . . a parrot feather or a Victorian key," you say, blurting the first things that come to mind, wanting to impress them.

"We are experts on freedom and expression—to represent this, we believe the magical object is a bird feather."

"No, no!" P. T. Barnum insists. "It has to be the key! A key is the symbol for unlocking the secrets of the living."

If you agree with the creatives and say that the magical object is a feather, turn to page 95.

If you agree with the entertainers and suggest that the object will be a key, turn to page 122.

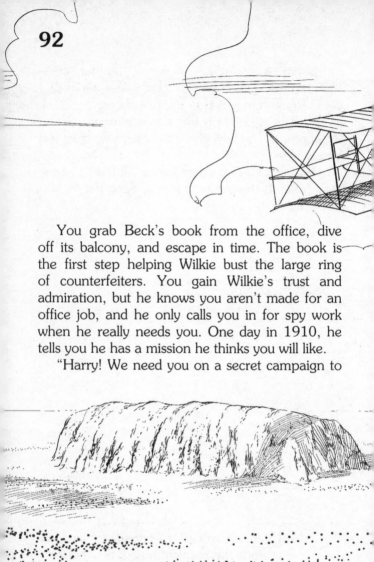

You grab Beck's book from the office, dive off its balcony, and escape in time. The book is the first step helping Wilkie bust the large ring of counterfeiters. You gain Wilkie's trust and admiration, but he knows you aren't made for an office job, and he only calls you in for spy work when he really needs you. One day in 1910, he tells you he has a mission he thinks you will like.

"Harry! We need you on a secret campaign to

promote the use of airplanes for defense," Wilkie explains. You are eager for the assignment to be one of the world's first pilots.

You are sent on another covert mission—to Australia. A Voisin plane is built for you. Everyone believes you are there to become the first person to fly in Australia. Your time Down Under proves you to be a skilled pilot. Yet, you crash. And survive. You are truly a superman.

The End

94

"Miiiii-awwww!" shrieks The Cat Woman when you approach her. Her skin is covered in tattoos of botanical plants, ancient texts, strange musical notes, pyramids, hieroglyphs, and other mysterious symbols. She seems to have real cat whiskers, furry ears, and a tail.

"What would you like to learn meow?" she asks you. You pummel her with questions; she answers like a wise oracle. She expertly teaches you methods for secret writing: how to use heat, chemicals, or light to create secret messages. You learn about codes, types of disappearing ink, and how to tattoo secret messages onto tricky surfaces.

She starts mewing and moaning, suggesting that cat song is its own code that cats used to rule in Egypt long time ago.

"Huh? I can't exactly understand you. I am not sure if I have learned all that you can from you . . . or if I have only scratched the surface!" you joke, but you are both frightened and enthralled.

"Give me your paw—I can meow-actually show you!" She insists, stretching her long nails outward to you. Her eyes are green and glowing.

If you're unsure of her and believe you are ready for bigger assignments, report back to Wilkie by turning to page 52.

To ask The Cat Woman to take you to Egypt, turn to page 113.

You side with the poets and choose the feather—for you adore birds. Indeed, you are able to contact your dear loved ones. You break through so far, in fact, that you appear back in your material body. The dead congratulate you as you leave. Earthside, you are embraced and called supernatural. You desperately try to feel normal, but you have seen too much. You decide it's time to face your most dangerous escape ever . . . Niagara Falls, the death wish.

"Don't do it! Let's use a stunt dummy!" your assistant, Bess, yells to you over the roaring water. You loom over the notorious Niagara Falls, ready to launch down and attempt the most dangerous feat ever. Your friends and even the movie producers filming all want you to rig the trick so you aren't really endangering yourself, but you resist.

You want it filmed to be included in a future movie, making you a screen star. You figure, what do you have to lose? You have already died once. "Don't be silly, I do my own stunts!"

You are nailed inside a wooden, reinforced barrel. This becomes your coffin. Still, it is the death you dreamed about, submerged at a super-human rate into an icy, majestic waterbody with everyone watching now and into the future.

The End

You absolutely refuse to listen to this nonsense. The medium agrees it is unsupportive and moves on to others' wishes. You leave, recommitted to the magic game. You collect a mountain of magic materials, teach other magicians you approve of, and reign as the president of the Society of Magicians.

The End

You find Bess in her dressing room.

"Bess, Bess, we must leave now—right now."

"Hooray! Harry, I am so ready to fly away from the chaos of Coney Island and my repetitive singing act!" she chirps.

You gather your trunk of tricks and costumes and take the steam train into the city. You lug the trunk around Grand Central Station, trying to decide where to go to perform. You buy a newspaper from a boy and open it up. You spot a Bloomingdale's department store ad offering a reward to any magician who can escape one of their packing crates. Just the ticket!

Turn to the next page.

98

The Packing Case Crate Escape at Bloomingdale's stands in the center of the entryway to the massive department store. Signs point to the large, wooden crate. When you step up to try the escape, you are inspected for secret tools. No one knows you have snuck a pick inside a fake thumb.

You successfully undo the hinges and emerge, triumphant. "Behold! I've escaped!" you announce to the crowd. "This silly crate is no container for my genius!"

The escape makes the front page of the papers, and you win a shopping trip. Bess buys clothing to alter for her spectacular costumes. You upgrade your wardrobe to include a top hat and tails. This boosts your confidence.

"It is time to do the Upside-Down Straight Jacket Escape!" you tell Bess.

"We can do anything," Bess agrees. You infiltrate Times Square with flyers announcing your next big trick. Bess helps find a crane and a crane operator. They park in front of a skyscraper, and an enormous crowd gathers. Bess laces you up in a straitjacket, which secures your arms across your chest, folded into your armpits, and wrapped and secured across your back. There is no way to reach the knots.

Turn to page 100.

"Whoa!" "Incredible!" "I can't believe it," the crowd below shouts as the crane lifts you and dangles you upside down ten stories above them. Many are immigrants who have just arrived at Ellis Island, and your stunt is their first experience of America. You and your escape talents are the ultimate symbol of freedom.

You start to jerk, whipping your body from left to right, your hair flapping, the crowd cheering, contracting your abdomen toward your knees, to create slack. You lift your arms overhead, so you can grab the buckle with your teeth, but you are caught in a tight squeeze. You didn't puff up enough when you were tied to make room for you to wiggle your arms overhead or to reach the knife you stuck under your arm.

It's time to *Houdinize* yourself, the word your fans use to describe your ability to get out of a tight spot. You could keep wiggling, or you could dislocate your shoulder, which you saw done at Coney Island and you've been practicing, but you aren't feeling confident about the maneuver in this position. What do you do?

If you devote all energy to wiggling, trying to reach the knife in your armpit, go on to the next page.

If you dislocate your shoulder to get out of the straitjacket and chains, turn to page 123.

You are already feeling beaten up, so you decide not to mess with your sockets. You wiggle and wiggle, feeling close to being able to grab the knife hidden in your armpit when you hear a *snap!* The crane's boom breaks and you drop.

"Uh-ohhhhhh!" you yell as you fall, feeling you have finally met life's end.

But your admiring fans below catch you. You crowd surf, bouncing back. You have never felt better at failure. The city still calls you "Miracle Man" in the papers when they describe the crane escape.

"Bess, we must do more stunts and shenanigans. I know! We will go up the Hudson and I will drop into the river, cuffed."

"My goodness, that is quite a lot of risk!" Bess reminds you.

"But I can hold my breath underwater for a *long* time."

"Harry, I am not sure I am cut out for this—what do you need me for?" she coos in her bird voice.

"I need you to lock me up! And greet the onlookers. C'mon, the papers will love it. Let's go, we can be up there by the afternoon to set up and alert the press."

Turn to the next page.

102

Your river escape draws thousands and garners successful press reports. Next, you escape out of a milk crate, then a crystal water closet, and several rectangular torture racks. Even when you are frozen, you can escape from a block of ice; then an iron coffin, a giant envelope, and so on until one day you are bored by boxes and traps.

"Bess, I am ready to catch a bullet."

"What? No! I swear, working for you is exciting, but I also feel like I am trapped myself, in Dante's Circles of Hell . . . only instead of nine levels, it is nine cubes! Nine cubes! Box after box-shape after box after box. I help you with your acts. But I will not stand by while someone shoots a bullet at you."

"How about burying me alive?"

"The Buried Alive Escape? Under six feet of dirt? I will quit if you do that, you have gone mad."

"But Bess, I am the best. I shall be the first to survive it, I have been practicing. Please, you cannot leave—everyone oohs and ahhs at your costumes! You are my good luck charm. Or I could do the Water Torture Cell?"

"Harry, what is that!"

"It's a see-through water tank, and I am locked by my ankles upside down inside. I am not sure what is more press-worthy at this point in my career."

Either way, it seems you will lose Bess as a friend and assistant. She storms off.

If you insist on doing the Water Torture Cell, turn to page 127.

Or you decide to be buried alive, turn to page 118.

A strange water beast has washed up on the Atlantic shore. Everyone gathers to rally you to escape from the inside, saying it will be just like the story of Jonah and the Whale.

"Watch me! I shall emerge from inside a huge belly of this ominous death-trap. The Water Beast has never before been attempted. Who knows what is inside there! Of course, I can conquer the mysteries of the deep sea! Sign me up!" you say.

However, inside the creature it is dark and suffocating. Ribs poke everywhere, and fumes of decay surround you. You will be triumphant but choke as you moan, trying to get out of your cuffs. Once you do and finally hit fresh air, you collapse but never come back. You've been poisoned.

The End

104

You confront your brother after your performances. He always joins you in the green room.

"How dare you!" you yell at Dash, and you sock him in the eye.

The door swings open and Melville rushes in. "Stop this!" he booms. "You two are brothers. That is a very special bond. Plus, we have very important work to do. Harry, we need you to break into the Kaiser's special safe, where he keeps his blueprints and plans for world domination."

"Say no more in front of my brother. Can we trust him?"

"Work it out, boys. Listen," Melville continues, "Wilhelm II will be hosting mock war games to show off his cavalry. He'll bring his horses and a lot of pomp, his warfare, and men. We need you to offer a private performance as a distraction. Not to worry, we will have the best cabinet built by our secret agent. He is already in the royal workforce as a welder. It will connect you to a series of tunnels to access their safe in their bank bunker of the castle compound."

You're thrilled and ready for something less redundant than busting imposters.

Go on to the next page.

When you set up for your private tented show, you witness a whole valley filled with horses and regalia. Alongside the fields are the appliances of modern warfare displayed for the attendees. It is quite the military spectacle procession! Wilhelm's army and his attitude are baffling. So boastful, but also frightening. You know there are secrets to expose.

Your show goes off without a hitch. Before you know it, you find yourself in the secret tunnels of the compound. Using the map from the inside agent, you discover a large treasury, where statues, ancient artifacts, Egyptian art, and jewels are stored.

Your mission is to take a set of blueprints that Melville is certain are in the safe. The blueprints hold the secrets to the Kaiser's most dangerous and experimental war machines.

Listening to its *chirrs* and *clicks* of the steel-cased safe, you master the lock. Success!

Turn to page 107.

You lift an Egyptian Pharaoh's headdress from a glass case and stare at it. The headdress is lined with lapis, emeralds, and gold. You put it on your head. You feel distinct powers rippling around your face. Whoa, this is what it is like to be a king, you fantasize.

But then, you hear footsteps. They could belong to a guard! The guards are so heavily armed here, you do not want a confrontation. The footsteps come right to the door. You quickly check the room for exits and decide your only choice is to step into the safe and lock yourself inside. It is large enough for you to fit, and you know how to open it from the inside.

You wait in the safe and hear security guards talking to each other. They don't seem to be in a hurry to leave. You were supposed to return quickly to the stage with the blueprints. If the guards do not leave soon so you can go back, your accomplices will be alarmed . . . and the mission may fail.

As you pull down the tubes of rolled blueprints, you notice there is an empty space behind the back wall of the safe. You move your hands all over and realize it leads you to a tunneled hallway where there is no floor. You are pulled in like a magnet but hope it may be a shortcut. Immediately, you are afloat.

Turn to the next page.

108

You float in darkness, without any awareness of time. You start to smell damp, moist walls. You must be in a subterranean passage in an underground lair.

Yet you are drawn toward a sliver of light refracting through an opening in the darkness.

Forces pull you into a hall of documents. Shelves of scrolls line walls that glitter with painted figures of Hathor-the-sky-goddess; Thoth, the magic-creator; Bast, the cat-ruler; Isis and Osiris. You remember from your magic studies that underneath the Sphinx in Egypt is the Hall of Records, a storehouse for all of the knowledge across all of eternity. Perhaps you have been transported to the greatest magic library ever.

"Oh, Thoth, what should I do? Why am I here?" you wonder aloud.

Do you try to grab one scroll, perhaps it will have better technology than the German blueprints? Turn to page 124.

If you leave the library of strange knowledge alone, turn to page 128.

"Phhhhraaaagumpf!" You vomit up the metal cutter that was encased in wax so it would not kill you. *Phew!* you think as you puke it safely into your hand. You unwrap it and pierce the zinc floor of the wagon. Peeling back the edges to reach the wood underneath is very difficult with such a small tool. The next part of your plan entails removing enough of the planking to enable you to squeeze through the floor.

You are triumphant.

"I am prisoner here," you report to your brother, and Melville. You do not hear back, for all communication is intercepted.

Instead, your success alerts Czar Nicholas, who adores you! He recruits you to be his advisor. You accept out of fear that if you don't comply, you will be eaten by rats in a Russian prison. So you go to live in the compound of "all-seeing," special people, there to entertain the Czar. It feels no different from your circus days. Only you cannot leave. Ever.

The End

110

"Stop the seance! These mediums are frauds. They are preying on you people, aching to hear from a loved one." Everyone is aghast. You shove the table hard with both hands, announcing: "These fakes scour everywhere for information. She must have read about me because I am so famous."

"Shh! You will scare off the spirits! They hate skeptics," Mystic O pleads.

You flip the table over. "See me ring the bell with my toes?" You reveal a rigged foot pedal.

"Beware, these fakies will act like salespeople to get into your house for family clues, study cemeteries, and read graves for information so they can pry and prey on your emotions. I know this because I do the same in my work on stage. It takes a flimflammer to catch a flimflammer."

Go on to the next page.

You make it your mission to debunk seance after seance. Determined to stop the Spiritualists, you use what you know of illusion tricks like mental distraction. You study for crookedness in the "contact" the mediums present as real: automatic writing, spirit photography, and slate board messages.

You add a whole act to your show where you lecture on the Spiritualists' fakery and expose their tricks. Recruiting helpers throughout the country, you create your own team of spies to infiltrate and break up seances. You dress up as a grieving, widowed man and show up to homes and hotels across the country to bust seances. Many livelihoods are ruined.

You take your mission all the way to Congress and create a national stir. Many practitioners want revenge.

Turn to the next page.

112

One night in Montreal, Canada, a few weeks into your huge North American tour, a man who claims to be a student barges into your dressing room. He slams your gut with a ferocious punch.

"You ruined my career!" he yells.

You have no chance to brace your abdomen and double over in searing pain as he flees the scene.

You refuse to stop performing and travel by train to Detroit, insisting it is just a pulled muscle. But during your last show in Detroit, your appendix ruptures. You have an infection inside an infection in your intestine. Your organs trick you—you think you are living, but every piece of you is shutting down. When the curtain falls, you fall to the floor. The audience thinks it is theatrics, but you are rushed to the hospital.

"I am done fighting," you lament. Always one with impeccable timing, you wait and suffer and finally die. It happens to be on Halloween.

The End

To attempt to live again, turn to page 87.

"You seem to know a lot about Egypt. Do you have a way to go there?"

"Only I know how to access the Land of Bast in Ancient Egypt."

"Um, like you can time travel?"

"Meow, of course. Follow me." She must be teasing you, but you are so curious. Coyly, she flicks her tail as she turns. Indeed, you follow her as she moves in between the canvas of attached tents. The maze of flaps is disorienting. The floor begins to wobble. *What am I doing?* you wonder. You try to grab her tail to get her attention—and to hold on to something as your jostle into flaps.

But, just like that—just like a cat—she darts off and is gone. The tent walls wrap you and then launch you up into the air as if on a trampoline, into what seems like nothingness.

Turn to page 108.

You pop the trunk lid open all the way and start to lift yourself out. You stand and face a hoard of hobos. "Who are you?" they snarl, showing few teeth, and emanating wrath of odors.

Surely, you can distract or de-escalate any bum. You make your presence known. "I am the Great Houdini!"

"We don't care. What are you doing here? Do you know the way of the hobo?"

You offer a magic coin trick from your pocket, hoping to distract them. The hobos are offended and now they've seen your coin stash . . . you have trespassed in their territory and seem too highfalutin to be trusted. They surround you. "These are fake coins, by the way . . . you could use them to fool others . . . uh and get out of poverty!" you add. It doesn't matter. They have knives, and hunger in their eyes.

The End

You decide the only way to get ahead of all the imposters and competition is to publish a catalog revealing all the secrets to your tricks. Your brother and friends try to stop you, distract you, even offering to buy you new tricks like disappearing an elephant or walking through a wall. You ignore them and publish a book called *My Master Secrets*, burning the ground for any future magician to replicate the magic. You hate copycats.

The End

You decline Melville's offer and decide to dedicate yourself to your act. Unfortunately, there is more and more competition and word of your failure spreads. Your chances at a comeback are ruined. You leave Europe in shame. When you try to revive your act in America, the European papers have broadcast tales of your failed shows all the way home.

You have no choice but to return to Wild Man status, which was a character you played coming up, where you were caged and painted your face like an animal. Playing "savage" is degrading, especially to the Indigenous people. The act is awful, and for once you feel suffocated. The "cage" of exploitation is one you can't ever escape. You die of humiliation.

The End

118

"Bury me alive! I will survive, unlike anyone before me," you shout to thousands of gawkers. You must keep upping your promises and tricks. You gather the finest team and the finest dirt to dig six feet deep into the earth. Extreme energy and breathing techniques are required.

"Soon, my voice will be muffled, and I will miss you!" you jest as dirt cascades on top of you, foot after foot. You create a pocket of air to use but become exhausted. The weight of the earth is killing you. Still, you wiggle your toes, thinking, *Just poke the little piggies burrowing in the mud.* Slowly, slowly, you create movement and are able to shift your limbs. Having such little oxygen clobbers you as you claw your way out. You finally are able to stick one hand out.

Go on to the next page.

Your assistants gather your arms and pull you out, only to find you utterly unconscious. You are the premiere Escapologist. Was this your greatest trick, or should you attempt a dangerous unknown extreme, escaping from a washed-up creature, The Water Beast?

If you decide it is time to wind down your career on a high note, turn to page 129.

If you decide it is time to escape from a water beast, turn to page 103.

"Dad, you are a religious man, and you have still managed to contact me from the beyond. This must be really important to you, and you must have knowledge from the afterlife. Even though I have been passionate and true to myself, I'd rather make you happy."

You leave the field of magic and return to Wisconsin to work for a locksmith. The friendly, small-town Midwest bores you after life as a fast-paced entertainer. Lock after lock, you look at each intricate mechanism, knowing their capacity for magic and to take down crime. At home, you cry for your old life.

The End

You agree to get in on the gambling riches. You know how to play trick cards and fool other players. You have to wear various disguises in order to continue to beat the top winners. Being a criminal has its perks!

You purchase a huge mansion in New York City for your family. Inside it, you create secret chambers, book collections on magic, and a museum of your accomplishments. Into a custom-made gigantic bathtub, you dump pounds of ice to train your body to withstand the cold in case you ever get to return to magic and escapes in an icy river act.

The End

You say it is safe to count on being summoned by a key. Every friend you have on the other side will think of keys when they think of you, and the many times you used them in your magic. But no one brings a key to the seance, so it does not trigger the channel to work. You try to send them messages with your mind. You can reach no one.

Soon you discover that you are an excellent spy from the other side. You spend an eternity haunting people and eavesdropping on their stories and observing their actions. Only this time you must report back to the Grand Architect.

The End

You jerk your shoulder out of its socket, just as you have done so many times before. It doesn't go back in when you descend. They have to cut the straitjacket off while you are still upside down. In fact, you've suffered a broken shoulder bone. It never heals. They have to amputate, putting a huge damper on your ability to unlock things. You still have your toes and your mouth, at least. You feel a phantom arm and it haunts you, however. You adjust to the pain and create a new life as The One-Shouldered Man.

The End

124

You pull a glowing scroll of text out from a shelf. "Mystery attracts mystery," you whisper.

Suddenly, there is a flash of light and monstrous noise erupts. Uh-oh. Mummies rise up from the cavernous walls. A curse! Wisps of apparitions swirl all around you, wrapping you in ancient cloth until you are a mummy they are burying in a tomb. What a way to go.

The End

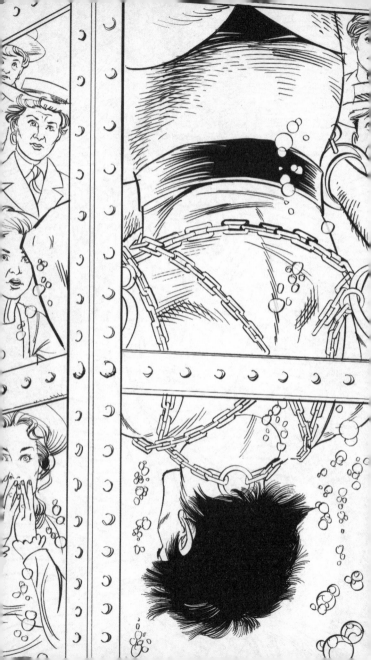

You have always wanted to escape the well-known but treacherous trick, the Water Torture Cell.

"How long can a man hold his breath underwater?" you ask the audience. "You're in luck, for I am a SUPER man! No shapes, no elements, no metals can stop me—just watch!"

Assistants secure you upside down by your ankles and shackle your legs and arms. They lift you into the tank, dangling. You have limited oxygen and must contort and shift your body and break your bonds. Water fills the tank, cooling your body. You start shifting, but there is so little room in the glass case. *I thought this would be stupendous,* you think, regretting it immediately.

The audience loves seeing you struggle, believing it is part of the act. You jerk quickly, panicking, as you run out of air. Your ankle breaks in the stocks above you. Searing pain absorbs you as you yell for help, bubbles signaling to the crowd that not all is well. Hammers come to break the glass, but . . .

The End

128

You are so inspired by the library, but do not want to invoke a curse by meddling. In the fullness of time, you amass an extensive collection of magic history, posters, ephemera, theater books; these you use in your own writing and articles. You are always learning. Your prized possession is a collection of *Weird Tales* magazines, which include the story "Under the Pyramids" by H. P. Lovecraft, your ghostwriter. It tells the tale of a man named Houdini who was captured and has to escape monsters under the Sphinx. Houdini does, of course, but insists it was all a dream. Or was it?

The End

You are beyond ready to rest your body and stop damaging it. But you are addicted to entertaining, and you believe you will be an exceptional silent film star. You can rest on your laurels and perform your stunts on film. You play a submarine inventor in *Terror Island*, a man who has been frozen in ice in *The Man from Beyond*. In *The Grim Game*, you survive an air collision and in *Haldane of the Secret Service*, you perform an incredible escape from a moving waterwheel.

You even have your own film company and invest a ton of money into launching Houdini Motion Pictures. Even though your films do not do all that well at the box office, your tricks now have a life of their own forever.

The End

You put your face next to the box and yell in at Beck. "I shall release you on one condition—that you share the *real* money with the performers."

"Yes, yes, it's in the safe, which I promise won't burn!"

You undo the hinges to release Beck. Fire engulfs the theater, but Beck shoves you down and laughs. All promises are off!

You die in the blaze. Your friends gather your ashes, cursing Beck, and vowing you are not really gone. The all-knowing fortune-teller from the show keeps some of your ashes with her in a pouch. One midnight on a full moon, she and your performer friends create a ritual to bring you back to life. They circle-dance around your ashes and light candles. She buries them and raises her arms to the moon. "You always have to beat the confines of the body. You shall be like a phoenix, an animal all magicians have forever admired for its ability to transform."

The End

The Story of Harry Houdini

The magician and showman famous around the world as Harry Houdini came to the United States as a young child, seeking a better life with his family. He was born in Budapest, Hungary, and his name was Erik Weisz.

Harry's family lived in Appleton, Wisconsin, where his father became rabbi of the Jewish congregation. They moved around the country and eventually settled in New York City, where Harry worked as a child. He earned money as a trapeze artist and locksmith before he was nine years old.

Becoming a great magician took many years of difficult practice. During the 1890s, when Harry began working as a magician, card tricks and wild stage acts were popular. People appeared as Strong Men or Sword Swallowers, wowing or frightening audiences with the unbelievable and the bizarre. As Harry became better and better at escapes, his fame grew.

Harry Houdini's longtime magician assistant, Bess Rahner, was also his wife. The two traveled all around the United States performing breathtaking stunts, all thanks to Harry's friend Martin Beck. Martin was Harry's manager, agent, and promoter. He gave Harry advice on his escape acts and booked him all over the United States in 1899.

In 1900, Harry toured the world as the "Handcuff King." His show was a hit. Houdini escaped from nailed packing crates, the belly of a whale, and barrels thrown over rivers. Historians believe it was during this time that he also began conversations with secret military operatives who enlisted Harry's brilliant mind and escape skills for work as a spy for Scotland Yard, relaying information to the British government from abroad, under the guise of traveling as a magician.

It's not always fun being famous. Houdini's fame sometimes created conflicts with other magicians, as well as the merchants that promoted him. He had many enemies and he made things worse by attacking them in the press or challenging them in unfair ways. He also had conflicts with the increasingly popular spiritualists, performers who traveled the country performing supernatural acts. They claimed to speak with the dead and use powers from other worlds for their tricks. Harry always claimed his magic was his alone. He even made an enemy of Sir Arthur Conan Doyle, the author of *Sherlock Holmes* and a fervent spiritualist, after Houdini started denouncing mediums that Conan Doyle genuinely believed were able to communicate with the dead.

Harry expanded his escapes to film in 1906, and became very interested in filmmaking. He worked on almost twenty films or serial film episodes (like television shows, but before television existed). He wanted to save his stunts as he performed them in front of audiences, especially those during which he was in the air, but he never became successful as an actor.

Harry also became a pilot, flying a French biplane in Germany. He went to Australia, hoping to be the first person in Australia to fly a plane. He was not, but his fame got him credit for it, and for many years he was falsely known as the first to fly in Australia.

Houdini died in 1926, when he was 52 years old, of a ruptured appendix. He had been struck in the abdomen days before by a student who was threatened by Houdini's abilities, and he'd already been in bad shape after breaking his ankle while performing. Houdini's body had seen many dangers and challenges in his years of performing, and we may never know exactly what chain of events brought him to the end of his life.

Harry's contributions to magic and his collections and papers continue to inspire people around the world today.

ABOUT THE ARTISTS

Illustrator: Eoin Coveney is an Irish illustrator who lives and works in Southern Ireland. After a couple of years in the UK and Germany working as a graphic designer, he returned to Ireland in the mid-'90s. For the last twenty-five years, he has been working with a diverse client base, on a wide variety of commercial projects. His aesthetic has been shaped by European comics, horror films, and early twentieth-century illustration. Early in his illustration career, he worked with Will Eisner (renowned comic creator and inventor of the term "Graphic Novel"). From this experience, he gained valuable insight into the process of telling stories through pictures.

Cover Artist: Mia Marie Overgaard has been working as a professional artist since graduating from the Royal Danish Academy of Architecture's School of Design in 2006. Mia's creative curiosity has allowed her to span a variety of media and creative fields—from illustration to fashion, graphic design, and fine art. Mia's distinctive illustrations have appeared in numerous books and publications worldwide, and have been exhibited in various locations around the globe such as London, Paris, Estonia, Georgia, Hungary, Sweden, Denmark, and Tokyo.

ABOUT THE AUTHOR

Katherine Factor is a writer, editor, and educator. She has worked as a writing coach and has instructed young writers at Idyllwild Arts Academy, Interlochen Arts Academy, and in summer programs. A graduate of the Iowa Writers' Workshop, her poems and other work can be found in print, audio, online, and at katherinefactor.com. *Harry Houdini* is her second *Choose Your Own Adventure* book. She is also the author of *Choose Your Own Adventure Spies: Mata Hari*.

For games, activities, and other fun stuff, or to write to Katherine, visit us online at CYOA.com

HARRY HOUDINI

This book is different from other books. YOU and you alone are in charge of what happens in this story.

You are Harry Houdini, a street performer who dreams of becoming the most famous magician in the world. You have been dazzling audiences and provoking police across the United States with your edgy escape acts. But you dream of even bigger glory.

The year is 1899, and you are approached by the head of the U.S. Secret Service with a special mission. Will YOU, Harry Houdini, agree to use your sleight of hand talents and your enormous intelligence to travel abroad and spy for the United States? And maybe find international fame when you are there? Or will you stay in America to perfect your tricks, with the help of your wild and diverse friends from Coney Island and San Francisco? You will also make choices that determine YOUR own fate in the story. Choose carefully, because the wrong choice could end in disaster—even death. But don't despair. At any time, YOU can go back and make another choice, and alter the path of your fate . . . and maybe even history.

VISIT US ONLINE AT CYOA.COM